TO OPEN

SAMUEL MENASHE

to
open

The Viking Press · *New York*

First published in 1974 by The Viking Press, Inc.
625 Madison Avenue, New York, N.Y. 10022
Published simultaneously in Canada by
The Macmillan Company of Canada Limited
SBN 670–71766–5
Library of Congress catalog card number: 73–17680

Acknowledgments are made to the editors
of the following periodicals,
in which some of these poems first appeared:
*The Antioch Review, The Berkeley Review, Commonweal,
Encounter, Genesis: Grasp, Harper's Magazine,
I.E., Invisible City, The Iowa Review, Midstream,
The New York Review of Books, The New Yorker,
The Poetry Review, The Times Literary Supplement,*
and *The Yale Review.*

The author wishes to express his thanks
to the MacDowell Colony in Peterborough, New Hampshire,
and to the Villa Serbelloni of the Rockefeller Foundation
in Bellagio (Como), Italy, where some of
these poems were made.
Printed in U.S.A.

CONTENTS

no jerusalem but this

The shrine whose shape I am
Has a fringe of fire
Flames skirt my skin

There is no Jerusalem but this
Breathed in flesh by shameless love
Built high upon the tides of blood
I believe the Prophets and Blake
And like David I bless myself
With all my might

I know many hills were holy once
But now in the level lands to live
Zion ground down must become marrow
Thus in my bones I'm the King's son
And through death's terrain I go
Making my own procession

Eaves at dusk
beckon us
to peace
whose house,
espoused,
we keep.

Wind

dabbles in grass
branches out
unravelling silk
from saplings

Stone would be water
But it cannot undo
Its own hardness
Rocks might run
Wild as torrents
Plunged upon sky
By cliffs none climb

Who makes fountains
Spring from flint
Who dares tell
One thirsting
There's a well

IN STRIDE

Streets at night like decks
With spars overhead
Whose rigging ropes
Stars into scope

My angels are dark
They are slaves in the market
But I see how beautiful they are

SHEEP MEADOW

French spoken
across the snow
on Sheep Meadow
evokes a very rich hour
of the Duke of Berry . . .
three men traversing
a field of snow—
one of them alone—
hedged by trees
on the south side
where the towers
of the city rise . . .
one of those hours
in early afternoon
when nothing happens
but time makes room

Small stones for the Temple

are as shapely as your toes
arrayed in a row
under that dome
whose buttress is bone

RURAL SUNRISE

Furrows erupt
like spokes of a wheel
from the hub of the sun—
the field is overrun—
no rut lies fallow
as shadows yield
plow and bucket
cart and barrow

Reeds rise from water

rippling under my eyes
Bullrushes tuft the shore

At every instant I expect
what is hidden everywhere

THE NICHE

The niche narrows
Hones one thin
Until his bones
Disclose him

A-
round
my neck
an amu-
let
Be-
tween
my eyes
a star
A
ring
in my
nose
and
a gold
chain
to
Keep me
where
You
are

*

PASCHAL WILDERNESS

Blue funnels the sun
Each unhewn stone
Every derelict stem
Engenders Jerusalem

PARADISE—AFTER GIOVANNI DI PAOLO

Paradise is a grove
Where flower and fruit tree
Form oval petals and pears
And apples only fair . . .
Among these saunter saints
Who uphold one another
In sacred conversations
Shaping hands that come close
As the lilies at their knees
While seraphim burn
With the moment's breeze

Pity us
by the sea
on the sands
so briefly

The friends of my father
Stand like gnarled trees
Yet in their eyes I see
Spring's crinkled leaf

And thus, although one dies
With nothing to bequeath
Enough love survives
To make us grieve

PASTORAL

The neighboring hill
Where lambs graze
Lies ample and still
In its own haze

APRIL

It is the sun that makes us smile
It is the sun and spring has come
Soon it will reach Norway
Her wooden villages wet
Laughter in each rivulet

MAY

Sky thrust from town
Vaults high towers
But comes down
To flowers

THE SANDERLING

[handwritten: PIPER]

The sanderling *[handwritten: piper]*
Scampers over sand
Advances, withdraws
As breakers disband

[handwritten: M.]

[handwritten: 12/20/79]

Each wave undergoes
The bead of his eye
He pecks what it tows
Keeps himself dry

On my birthday

I swam in the sea our mother
naked as the day I was born
still fit at forty-four
willing to live forever

O Many Named Beloved
Listen to my praise
Various as the seasons
Different as the days
All my treasons cease
When I see your face

SHADE

Branches spoke
This cupola
Whose leaf inlay
Keeps the sun at bay

Roads run forever
Under feet forever
Falling away
Yet, it may happen that you
Come to the same place again
Stay! You could not do
Anything more certain—
Here you can wait forever
And rejoice at your arrival

DESCENT

My father drummed darkness
Through the underbrush
Until lightning struck

I take after him

THE PROBE

Who stands above this bed
Submits to scrubbed hands
Someone almost dead
A body none commands
Disorganized, below
That uniform whose probe
Compels flesh and bone
To show what is known

She who saw the moon last night
She who swayed with the chant
Died in her sleep or dreams
To say she is dead seems scant.

PIRATE

Like a cliff
My brow hangs over
The cave of my eyes
My nose is the prow of a ship

I plunder the world

These stone steps

bevelled by feet
endear the dead
to me as I climb
them every night

SELF EMPLOYED

Piling up the years
I awake in one place
and find the same face
Or counting the time
since my parents died—
certain less is left
than was spent—
I am employed
every morning
whose ore I coin
without knowing
how to join
lid to coffer
pillar to groin—
each day hinges
on the same offer

TENEMENT SPRING

Blue month of May, make us
Light as laundry on lines
Wind we do not see, mind us
Early in the morning

SOMEONE WALKED OVER MY GRAVE

The breath breaks a cold shuddered hollow
That instant, unbearably, I know
The beauty of this world

Those lips the young man my father
Found more fair than the bud of a rose
Now almost touched to dust—kiss that dust
You trod God of life, God of the world

SUNSET, CENTRAL PARK

A wall of windows
Ignited by the sun
Burns in one column
Of fire on the lake
Night follows day
As embers break

AUTUMN

I walk outside the stone wall
Looking into the park at night
As armed trees frisk a windfall
Down paths which lampposts light

NOVEMBER

Now sing to tarnish and good weathering
A praise of wrinkles which sustain us
Savory as apples whose heaps in attics
Keep many alive through old winter wars

PROMISED LAND

At the edge
Of a world
Beyond my eyes
Beautiful
I know Exile
Is always
Green with hope—
The river
We cannot cross
Flows forever

Red glints in black hair

It is the rose below white
Gold suns under sea green
A nose formed for insight
And all the visible not seen
Keeping my eyes to the king
As I call wise night my queen

CARNIVAL

Faces flowing up the street
Faces glowing to the feast
Great is the god they greet
Face to face, feet to feet

ENCLOSURE

Hagia Sophia's high dome
magnifies and confines
the mind's eye, home
within oval lines

JUDGMENT DAY

Aroused by smoke
We blunder out
Stone towers float
Loud trumpets sound
Among empty houses
Running men collide
None has found
Where to die

WARRIOR WISDOM

Do not scrutinize
A secret wound—
Avert your eyes—
Nothing's to be done
Where darkness lies
No light can come

TO OPEN

Spokes slide
Upon a pole
Inside
The parasol

A flock of little boats
Tethered to the shore
Drifts in still water
Prows dip, nibbling

White hair does not weigh

more than the black
which it displaces—
Upon any fine day
I jump these traces

The apple of my eye

now goes to seed
Wrinkles undermine
a dwindling cheek
No kiss ekes out
the stemmed mouth

Only the nose
does not shrink

SUDDEN SHADOW

Crow I scorn you
Caw everywhere
You'll not subdue
This blue air

Using the window ledge
as a shelf for books
does them good—
bindings are belts
to be undone
Let the wind come—
hard covers melt
Welcome the sun—
an airing is enough
to spring the lines
which type confines
But for pages uncut
rain is a must.

The hollow of morning
Holds my soul still
As water in a jar

A pot poured out
Fulfills its spout

PEACEFUL PURPOSES

Those flapping flags
That the wind cracks
Over the house
Like an attack
Might have been
Potato sacks
If dipped in
Another vat.

The water
of the world
is love

The Water
of the World
is Love

FEEDBACK

Stills of you
Splice the reel
Whose spool
They peel

DREAMS

What wires lay bare
For this short circuit
Which makes filaments flare—
Can any bulb resist
Sockets whose threads twist
As fast as they are spun—
Who conducts these visits
Swifter than an eclipse
When the moon is overcome?

WINTER

I am entrenched
against the snow,
visor lowered
to blunt its blow

I am where I go

FASTNESS

I shoulder the slope
which holds me
up to the sun
with my heels
dug into dust
older than hills

If I were as lean as I feel
only my bones would show
living bone, ideal—
without a shadow—
for the exacting dance
that the law commands
until I overstepped
the forbidden ark
to take on flesh
wrestling in the dark

THE MOMENT OF YOUR DEATH

My head bounces away
In the trough of a wave
You are unbound on your bed
Like water far from a shore
Nothing can reach you now
Not my kiss, not a sound
You are out of hearing
And I have run aground
Where gravel grinds
The face it blinds

SHEEN

Sun splinters
in water's skin
quivers hundreds
of lines to rim
one radiance
you within

THE BARE TREE

*My mother once said to me, "When one sees the tree in
leaf one thinks the beauty of the tree is in its leaves,
and then one sees the bare tree."*

1

Now dry stone holds
Your hopeful head
Your wise brown eyes
And precise nose

Your mouth is dead

2

The silence is vast
I am still and wander
Keeping you in mind
There is never enough
Time to know another

3

Root of my soul
Split the stone
Which holds you—
Be overthrown
Tomb I own

4

Darkness forged
Becomes a star
At whose core
You, dead, are

5

I will make you a landscape
Spread forth as waves run

After your death I live
Become a flying fish

DUSK

Voices
rise
from
earth
into
night

IMAGE

Sealed as the eye
Within its socket,
Bound by skull bone
I see you yet

Alone as the wind
Howling in a place
Where no one passes

EPITAPH

New deaths surround
Me step by step
Until I'm found
Engraved near you

One become two

O Lady lonely as a stone—
Even here moss has grown

CARGO

Old wounds leave good hollows
Where one who goes can hold
Himself in ghostly embraces
Of former powers and graces
Whose domain no strife mars—
I am made whole by my scars
For whatever now displaces
Follows all that once was
And without loss stows
Me into my own spaces

VOYAGE

Water opens without end
At the bow of a ship
Rising to descend
Away from it

Days become one
I am who I was

Sleep

gives wood its grain
dreams knot the wood

All things that heal
salve, herb, balm
goodness I feel
established calm

What form is as fair
as sunlight in air
as poultice to skin
thorns instantly tear

DREAMING

Windswept
as the sea
at whose ebb
I fell asleep,
dreams collect
in the shell
that is left,
perfecting it.

AWAKENING FROM DREAMS

Flung inside out
The crammed mouth
Whose meal I am
Ground, devoured
I find myself now
Benignly empowered

MY MOTHER'S GRAVE

Bones
Are mortar
For your wall

Jerusalem

Dust
Upholds
Your street

The shrine whose shape I am
Has a fringe of fire
Flames skirt my skin

enclosure

DAILY BREAD

I knead the dough
Whose oven you stoke
We consume each loaf
Wrapped in smoke

MANNA

Open your mouth
To feed that flesh
Your teeth have bled
Tongue us out
Bone by bone
Do not allow
Man to be fed
By bread alone

"And He afflicted thee and suffered thee to hunger and fed
thee with manna which thou knewest not, neither did thy
fathers know, that He might make thee know that man does not
live by bread alone, but by every word that proceeds from the
mouth of the lord does man live."

Deuteronomy VIII 3

The sea staves
Concave waves

That dream which escapes

As I, transported, wake
Leaves me no time to take
Into the sudden space
Day breaks upon my face

I am flashed back
Without warning
Taken by storm
Every morning

LANDSCAPE

Boughs berserk
Spin one hill
Into space
Standing still
Olive trees race

On the field below
Moulded white oxen
Ponder each furrow
A man behind them
Cries *Via, Via*

Leah bribed Jacob
With mandrake roots
To make him
Lie with her

You take my poems

MOON NIGHT

Old stones glow still on a path
Below the wall of the town
I see them and I love
Clear and whole
And so well
No ghosts
Groan at the gate
I am the tale they tell
Now without wind or word Know
This night is one and does not end
Only the day dreamers go

The hill I see
Every day
Is holy

As the tall, turbaned
Black incense man
Passed the house
I called after him
And ran out to the street
Where at once we smiled
Seeing one another
And without a word
Like a sword which leaps from its lustrous sheath
He was swinging his lamp with abundant grace
To my head and to my heart and to my feet . . .
Self-imparted we swayed
Possessed by that One
Only the living praise

Between bare boughs
One star decrees
Winter clarity

Pan's work is done
When grown men
Become wanton
As children
Who leap and run
Through green country
Seizing all they see

Walking under
Trees which tower
Gives feet ground
Boughs embower

LAMENT

Clouds before night flow near
Swallowing me now like snow
Soundless into swollen sea
Wind of ice, howl through me

Yet blithely but a moon ago
You laughed upon the tide
Cast me where I will not know
Let lilies heal my side

Like a gutted house
I am burned out
By love

FALL

Dry leaves fly
down the stream
you walked by

Near the water
I want to die

PAIN

Pain finds its place
Invades each vein
Whose lines trace
You in pain

Although

flowers seem better
than bread to cast
upon the water,
the dead outlast
whatever we offer

AUBADE

Wind stirs up palms
To stars becalmed
In sky where blue
Now ripples through

Near still white villas
Sprays undulate
Watering lawns
Where day now dawns

Whitewall away
Rundown stonestairs
Before the sun
To hut and prayers

Great Babylon
Dwarfs the sky
Her uproar
Swarms so high
The orb of the sun
Adorns Babylon

IDOL

Worship the swollen
Scrotum of the god
Strong men come
From this pod

I left my seed in a grove so deep
The sun does not reach through the trees
Now I am wed to the wood and lord of all leaves
And I can give the green blessing to whom I please

So they stood
Upon ladders
With pruning hooks
Backs to the king
Who took his leave
Of gardening

This morning
I am forlorn
As he was then
No one born
After the war
Remembers when

I lie in snows
Drifted so high
No one knows
Where I lie

As a stick that divines
I abruptly discover
In a tug of war
The arms of a lover

LE LAC SECRET

They have now traced me to my uncles
One died a beggar in a room with no windows
And one danced until he was undone, like Don Juan
Though they try to find me out, I am still as the swan
While those who search grow grim
And darker in their doubt

LINEAGE

Who will pity her
When she is so old
She cannot scold—
Not that son
Her tears dun—
Who then will
Be merciful—
No, no one
Called *Daughter*—
Her own grandson
Shall kiss her
Empty mouth

FOR ONE SLAIN

A stone of grief
Impounds the heart
Heavy, scarred

OLD MIRROR

In this glass oval
As love's own lake
I discover your face
Doubling my intake,
Beheld at each breath,
Of life before death

SIMON SAYS

In a doorway
Staring at rain
Simple withstands
Time on his hands

The room of my friend
Is a violet chapel
Where in pale state he lies
And daydreams dapple
His blue eyes

OUT OF THE DEPTHS

Like a dragnet
In whose mesh
Captives writhe
Water wrinkles
Increasing light . . .
A gap opens
You appear,
Dredged here.

In moonlight

Each face portrays
Itself become
Luminous

We do not speak
No tongue betrays
Our fluent feet

THE HEARTH

Love and hate
Fluctuate
As fire flames
Ash remains

The scrutiny
Of a chicken's eye
Terrifies me—
What does it think?
Not brain but beak
Chills my blood—
It stares to kill

SONG

The round moon is out
The night is cold and clear
I have not been found
Since my twentieth year

FIRE DANCE

Must smiles subside in a sigh
And sobs underlie laughter
Shall we always leap high
With flames leaping after

Just now

With my head down,
Bent to this pen
Which is my plow,
I did not see
That little cloud
Above the field—
Unfurrowed brow,
You are its yield

Gray boulder
Beside the road
You devote me to age
Whose date none decodes
From signs of fire or ice—
Elephant among field mice
You crouched here alone
In the silence of stone

All my friends are homeless
They do not even have tents
Were I to seek a safe place
I would run nights lost
Ice pelting my face
Sent the wrong way
Whenever I ask—
Afraid to turn back,
Each escape the last

Lie down below trees
Be your own guest
Give yourself up . . .
Under this attentive pine
Take your time at noon
The planes will drone by soon

PEACE

As I lie on the rock
With my eyes closed
Absorbed by the sun
A creak of oarlocks
Comes into the cove

CLAIR DE LUNE

This lunar air
Draws me to you,
The moon's magnet
Aligns that pair
Whom dragons slew,
Whose course was set
Before they knew

I am the hive
You inhabit
Celled inside
Me you multiply